The Wolf
Who Wanted to Be an Artist

Text by Orianne Lallemand
Illustrations by Eleonore Thuillier

AUZOU

It was a fine summer morning. The birds were singing, the breeze was gently blowing, and the flowers were in bloom. And the wolf was daydreaming near a waterfall.

Inspire us, young artists!
OL

"What are you doing, Wolf?"
asked Mr. Owl.

"I'm admiring the scenery," replied
the wolf. "It's so beautiful!"
"Oh," said Mr. Owl. "So you're
an **artist** now!"

Me? thought the wolf. *An artist?*
"Come to think of it," exclaimed the wolf.
"I've always wanted to **paint**. And I've got talent!"

So the wolf bought a canvas, an easel, and some tubes of paint.
He set up in the shade of an oak tree and went to work!

As he was working, Mrs. Wolf approached. "What are you up to, Mr. Wolf?" she asked. "I'm painting," replied the wolf. "The colors of the forest and the sound of the waterfall are an inspiration!"

Mrs. Wolf looked at the canvas. She saw a lot of purple
and a lot of blue.
"Mr. Wolf," she said. "I'm sorry to say, but I don't think
you're the most talented of painters. But you'll always be
my precious poet!"

"Mrs. Wolf is right," exclaimed the wolf. "I have the soul of a poet!"
He found a pencil and some paper, sat down, and started writing.

How enchanting is this summer's day
It really takes my breath away...

The wolf thought hard but couldn't think of anything else to write.
"Mr. Wolf," said a voice. "Why are you sitting as still as a statue?"
The wolf jumped up.
"A **sculptor**!" the wolf shouted. "I'll be a very talented sculptor."

Miss Yeti volunteered to pose for Mr. Wolf. So they went to his garden where the wolf carefully shaped the clay in his paws. When he finished, the wolf admired his work.
"Come and have a look," he told Miss Yeti.

Miss Yeti took one look at
the statue and flinched.
"I look like an elephant!"
she cried.
"You have absolutely
no talent as a sculptor,
you funny wolf."

She trampled the statue before disappearing into the forest.

"Funny wolf?" he repeated.
"I am a **comedian**!
I do love making people laugh!"

The cheerful wolf set up a stage in the forest and rehearsed for his show.
The passers-by were so fascinated by what he was doing, they stopped to listen.

Unfortunately, nobody laughed
at the wolf's jokes.
In fact, he was booed off stage
before the end of his show.

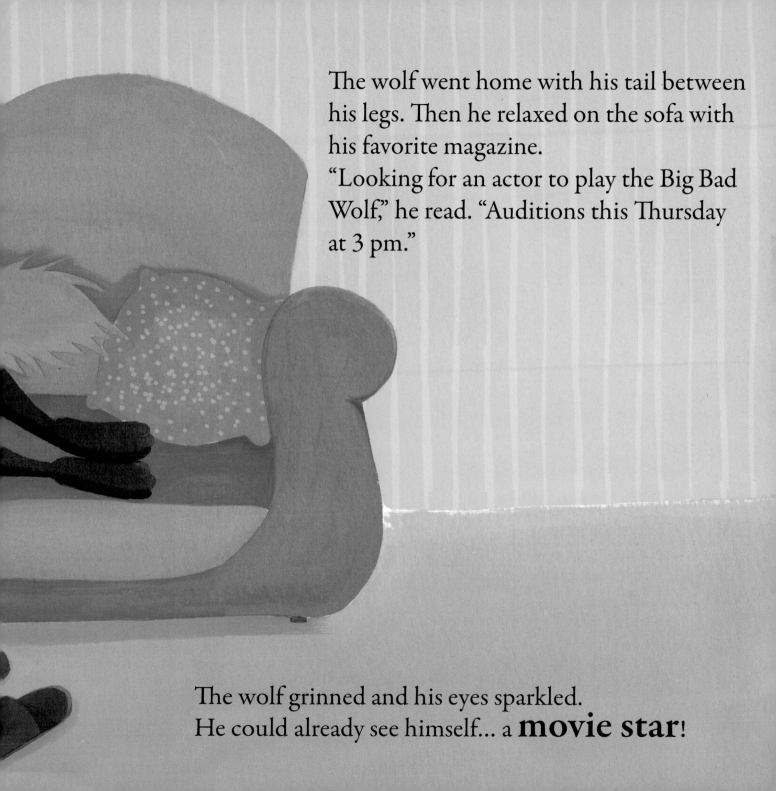

The wolf went home with his tail between his legs. Then he relaxed on the sofa with his favorite magazine.
"Looking for an actor to play the Big Bad Wolf," he read. "Auditions this Thursday at 3 pm."

The wolf grinned and his eyes sparkled.
He could already see himself... a **movie star**!

The next day, the wolf made sure he was on time for the audition. But when he opened the door the wolf had the fright of his life. "AAAHHHHHH!" he howled. "Those wolves are terrifying!"

The producer heard his howls and showed the wolf into his office.
"What a voice, dear friend, what a voice," declared the producer.
"You should be a singer. You'd be all the rage!"
"Oh, thank you," said the wolf. "I have always loved singing!"

The wolf rushed home and announced the news to his friends.
"I'm going to be a **rock star**," he told them.
"Who wants to be in my band?"

"Me!" shouted Big Louis. "I'll be the drummer!"
"And I can play the saxophone," said Alfred.
"I'm a great musician!" declared Valentino. "I can play the electric guitar!"
"And I can write the songs," suggested Joshua.

"What about us?" asked Mrs. Wolf and Miss Yeti.
"My little treasures," replied the wolf. "You will be our backup singers."

"And I'll be the lead singer," said the wolf.
"I have an incredible voice. Listen!"
And he started singing. His friends were stunned.
Mr. Wolf really did have talent!

lalalalalaaaa

"We'll meet here tomorrow,"
the wolf told his friends.
"Bring your instruments.
And when we've rehearsed,
we'll put on a concert!"

The band was named, The Rocking Wolves. They wrote the songs, composed the music, and set up the lighting and sound on the stage. Most importantly, they rehearsed every day.

When everything was ready for the concert, they put up posters
all over the forest. "*Open invitation for The Rocking Wolves concert.
Fantastic music and a great time guaranteed!*" they read.

The big night arrived at last.
The wolf made his entrance.
He took a deep breath
and started singing.
At the end of the first song,
there was complete silence.
And then a thunder of
applause exploded.
"One more, one more!"
shouted the animals.
Phew! The wolf sighed
with relief.
The band lit up the stage
and their concert was
an amazing success.

The next day, The Rocking Wolves were on the front page of all the newspapers. And they were invited to play in Paris, New York, and Rio!

Planet Music

"I've always been an artist at heart"

The Wolf Leader of the Rocking Wolves

Exclusive interview

The wolf replied to all the invitations:
"Thank you, you're very kind," he said.
"It's great being a **star** but I have so
many other things to do here at home."

General Director: Gauthier Auzou
Senior Editor: Laura Levy
English Version Editor: Rebecca Frazer
Layout: Annaïs Tassone
Translation from French: Susan Allen Maurin
Original title: *Le loup qui voulait être un artiste*
© Auzou Publishing, Paris (France), 2014 (English version)
ISBN: 978-2-7338-2703-1

Printed and bound in China, December 2013.